Morgan Robertson

A Tale of a Halo

Morgan Robertson

A Tale of a Halo

ISBN/EAN: 9783337090333

Printed in Europe, USA, Canada, Australia, Japan

Cover: Foto ©Andreas Hilbeck / pixelio.de

More available books at **www.hansebooks.com**

A TALE OF A HALO

BY

MORGAN A. ROBERTSON

ILLUSTRATED BY

A. CAREY K. JURIST

———

NEW YORK

THE TRUTH SEEKER COMPANY

28 LAFAYETTE PLACE

1894

A TALE OF A HALO.

St. Peter was gazing one day by the gate
At a sign on the rampart, and, sad to relate,
His face wore a look of surprise and chagrin,
For the sign bore the legend, "No Smoking Within."
While Peter was dozing a cherub had passed
And high on the rampart had made the sign fast;
For the Heaven-born privilege he had abused,
And the smoke from his pipe was through Heaven diffused.
And the smoke from that pipe had a smell of its own,
Too strong for the incense that hung 'round the Throne.

Then he picked up his pipe, his tobacco and stool
With a grunt of disgust at the new-fangled rule,

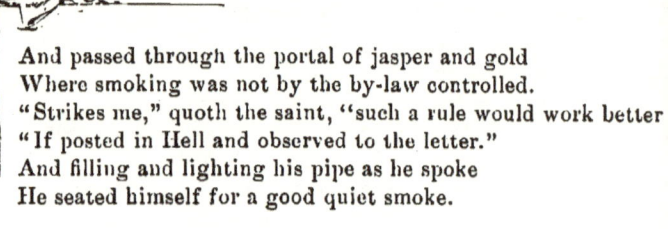

And passed through the portal of jasper and gold
Where smoking was not by the by-law controlled.
"Strikes me," quoth the saint, "such a rule would work better
"If posted in Hell and observed to the letter."
And filling and lighting his pipe as he spoke
He seated himself for a good quiet smoke.

As he smoked and reflected he noticed how cool
It seemed to be getting.   He picked up his stool
And moved somewhat nearer the gate to secure
What little warmth came from within: to be sure
He might, had he chosen, have broken the rule
And finished his smoking inside, but no fool
Was grizzled old Peter; he knew a complaint
Might give his position to some other saint.
So he smoked on in silence while colder it grew,
So cold that around his gaunt figure he drew
His robe a bit closer and swallowed the whole
Of the stem of his pipe to get warmth from the bowl.

"A cold wave is coming," said Peter at last.
"I hope there is nothing amiss with the blast

2

"In the regions below; for if Satan should bank
"His fires for a while, I am sure such a prank
"Would cause a revolt in the heavenly host,
"And not a soul here would remain at his post.
"For Hell is contrived on a plan so complete
"That the roasting of sinners shall furnish us heat.
"But singers can't sing when their lips are all chapped,
"And harpers are helpless with fingers enwrapped
"In mittens and gloves, and I very much doubt
"If anyone here could be very devout
"Or happy till Satan relighted the coals
"And started again the cremation of souls.
"My goodness, it's cold! I must go and inquire
"To see if there's anything wrong with the fire.

"I'll send down a message.   Hello, what is this?
"A spirit of earth! I perceive how it is,
"He brings the cold with him; no doubt on the earth
"This man was of consequence, noble in birth—
"I can tell by the cut of his jib. I suppose,
"To judge by his walk, he has come to foreclose

3

"A mortgage on Heaven, or maybe his nerve
"Is only sufficient to cause him to serve
"A writ of replevin to get the return
"Of the treasure he's laid up in Heaven: I'll learn.

"Ho, spirit of earth! now, before you advance
"Any farther, just tell me, to what lucky chance
"You owe your escape from the highroad to Hell!
"What name do you answer to? Where did you dwell?
"And what have you done in your earthly career
"To induce you to think you are welcome up here?"

The stranger he spoke to was tall and erect,
And his features were stamped with a haughty respect
For himself, so of course no attention he paid
To the saint, neither seemed he to think that his aid
Was in any way needful. He strode to the gate
Where he knocked long and loud, till he knocked off a plate
Of the jasper; and Peter, appalled and aghast
At the foul desecration, cried, "Hold, there! avast!
"Are you trying to enter fair Heaven by storm?
"You will hardly succeed: if you do not conform

4

"To the rules and reply to my questions, you'll find
"That you'll stay where you are till you've made up your
    mind."

The stranger now turned and regarded the saint
Severely and long; then with rare self restraint
Said, "Pardon me, sir; who is this I address?"
"St. Peter, and I am the——" "Wait, you digress.
"For all that I asked was your name, and you say
"St. Peter: now with your permission I may
"Inquire of you what are your duties up here."
"My duties are mainly to keep Heaven clear
"Of dead-heads, impostors and people like you
"Who I think would be better——" "Tut, tut, that will do.

"Your name is St. Peter: your duty, I find,
"Is to keep out the people whom you are inclined
"Or pleased to term dead-heads, impostors and such.
"This being the case, I yet doubt very much
"That you can consistently fail to concede
"That the converse is equally true, and you need

5

" At times to admit to the City within
" All such as are worthy of entrance therein.

" Am I right?" " I suppose so, but really can't see
" What you're driving at; what is your name?" " Pardon me,
" I will further continue. We reach, if you please,
" A point where your answer quite fully agrees
" With logic and reason. Now this much I find,
" As explaining your zeal and your rather unkind
" And intemperate speech, that you cannot conceal
" That you hold the Keys and the Heavenly Seal.

" This is so, is it not?" " Yes, it is," said the saint;.
" But I'm rather inclined to opine that you ain't
" A-going inside till——" " Excuse me, dear sir;
" Let me say that in grammar you carelessly err,
" As 'ain't' is a word that is seldom now heard
" From people of culture; 'tis hardly a word,
" But a union or vulgar corruption of two;
" And neither in fact in your sentence would do,
" Which, besides, in construction is very confused;
" And 'opine' is a word that is better not used.

6

"Your final remark was uncalled for indeed.
"But this is irrelevant: we will proceed
"With the question in hand. I have found the gate locked;
"I am anxious to enter; my feelings are shocked
"By your language and manner. Now, you have the key;
"Please attend to your duty." "Why, yes—but you see,
"I must ask you if——" "There, sir, we cannot debate
"Any longer this question: please open the gate!"

St. Peter, impressed by his manner and tone,
Was loth to commit himself. Once he had known
That trouble could follow the little word "No":
When the Archangel Michael had flown down below
On a tour of inspection in Hell, and a flame
Had singed off his wings so that downward he came
To the ground, which he struck with the back of his neck
(It took twenty devils to clear up the wreck),
And painfully homeward had wandered on foot,
With his face covered over with bruises and soot,
And the stumps of his pinions concealed by a part
Of his raiment which made him a fair counterpart

7

Of a hunchback; for Peter could not understand
How any such creature should dare to command
That he open the gates.   He declared he would not,
And well he remembered the thrashing he got.

With this in his mind it is not very strange
That he wavered and thought it was better to change
His tactics a little, for if he should make
Such a foolish, unseemly and grievous mistake
As to stop or annoy one of Heaven's elect,
Or treat him with any pronounced disrespect,
He *might* get in trouble, since many complaints
Of his conduct were made by the rest of the saints.

So the stranger's command he resolved to obey:
He ushered him in: then he pointed the way
To the outfitting office where, hanging on hooks,
Were the outfits for incoming souls.   There were books
Containing the anthems, hosannas and songs;
There were cymbals and harps for the worshiping throngs;
There were robes; there were crowns; there were halos so bright
As to dazzle the eye with their splendor and light;

8

And with these the newcomers were always supplied
The very first thing after getting inside.

The spirit in charge was remarkably kind
In his manner, and also polite and refined
Compared with St. Peter.   His life on the earth
Had been saddened with grief from the hour of his birth.
He had driven a car for a living, and this
Had earned him the right to a future of bliss.
For patience and sweetness of soul are by far
The greatest things needed in driving a car.
He never in life had been known to complain
Of his lot; but in sickness and sorrow and pain
Had held to his duty and nobly had tried
To reach his ideal of life, but he died.
He died, and the world never missed him at all:
He fell as a leaf in the autumn will fall.
But Heaven remembered and gave him the post
Of outfitting clerk to the heavenly host.

And this was the character, gentle and good,
Who welcomed the stranger and did what he could

9

To equip him completely. I will not detail
All the points of this interview—language would fail.
Suffice it to say that he criticised all
That the outfitter showed him; the halos were "small
And dull," and the crowns, though of finest of gold,
Were "loud and not high enough, shabby and old."

Though the robes were creations of beauty and taste,
And cut from the pattern of those which had graced
The forms of the angels since Heaven began,
The outfitting clerk was requested to plan
Him a new one, made up in a different style.
He would "wait there until it was ready"; meanwhile
He would "look at the harps." So he sampled them all.
They were "all out of tune, and besides rather small
In their compass"; and he had been wont to aspire
In his "musical efforts full three octaves higher."

He looked through the hymn-books and found that he knew
"By heart all the anthems," and also a few
That were very much better, and this would suffice,
For should he forget them he might improvise.

10

He needed no hymn-book, but as for the rest
Of his outfit, he wanted it " made by the best
Of the workmen and tailors that Heaven contained.
And to order" : but here was a hitch; there remained
. Not one of that skillful and dexterous band
Of angel mechanics whose genius had planned,
And gathered, and built from the chaos of Night
This beautiful, glorious City of Light;
And also had furnished some outfits for souls
Who could capture a place on the heavenly rolls.

For ages ago they had shown their dislike
Of working so hard and had gone on a strike
Under Satan, but failed in their object for, well,—
They all became devils residing in Hell.
Since then when the angels or spirits had done
Any damage in Heaven, a cherub would run
With a notice to Satan, who'd rout from their lairs
Some devils and send them to make the repairs.
And the devils by this time had mended the gate
Where the stranger had carelessly knocked off the plate.

11

All this was explained him: he was "in no haste,"
He wanted "an outfit that suited" his taste.
So, after much trouble, the outfitting clerk
Sent Satan the order, and Hell went to work.

It didn't take long with the skill at command
To finish and send up the goods, which were scanned
By the stranger with careful and critical eye.
He remarked that the crown was a "trifle too high."
And he asked for some acid to test it, "because,
Unless it were purest of metal," he was
"Not going to wear it": he found it all right;
But Hell got it back to reduce it in height.

He tried on the robe and he thought it "might do."
It was not what he wanted, but then it was "new,"
And that was "a point in its favor": the harp
Was a marvel of skill, but in no case would sharp;
It needed retuning, so Hellward it went.
But at sight of the halo his *hauteur* unbent
And his features relaxed to a jubilant gaze;
For here was a grand combination of rays

12

That spread from a circle with shimmer and sheen.
It baffles description; there never was seen
In Heaven such color and brilliant effect.
It would make him " the envy of all the elect."

The harp and the crown were returned very soon.
The crown was all right and the harp was in tune.
And then he accepted and found it the best
And handsomest outfit in Heaven possessed,
And quite to his liking, he said, "were it not
For a strong smell of brimstone pervading the lot."
But this would "wear off": he extended his thanks
To the outfitting clerk, then he left for the ranks
Of the choir; while the clerk, with a pain in his head,
Resigned his position and took to his bed.

In the meantime, the puzzled St. Peter had spent
Some moments in thinking, and then he had sent
A message to Michael explaining the case—
That a stranger had got through the gate "on his face."
The Archangel Michael was not to be found;
He was not in his office but "somewhere around,"

13

And the messenger searched in each cranny and nook
And found him at last overhauling the book
Of the angel in charge of the records, to learn
What Peter on earth had accomplished, to earn
His canonization; and who made the pleas
That put him in charge of the heavenly keys.

The Archangel Michael had ever remained
The handsomest angel that Heaven contained.
IIis face had the glory which righteousness brings,
And also, alone of the angels, his wings
Were made of asbestos—his mishap below
Had blistered the stumps and no feathers would grow.
And Michael could never get over the spite
IIe felt for the saint since the day of the fight;
For Peter, though whipped, had delivered some blows
With telling effect on the Archangel's nose.

Since then the Archangel had joined with the saints
Who envied St. Peter, and pushed the complaints
Of his scandalous pranks, that had gone to the Throne.
For 'round about Heaven 'twas very well known

14

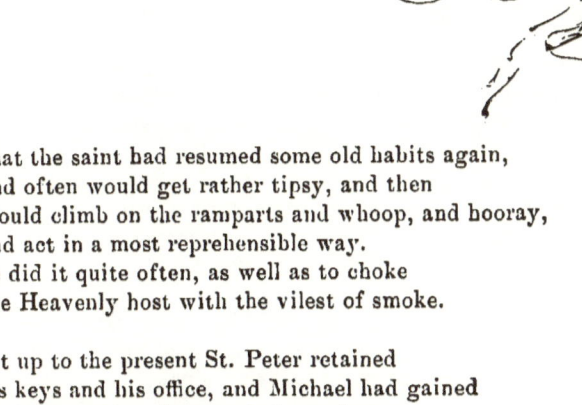

That the saint had resumed some old habits again,
And often would get rather tipsy, and then
Would climb on the ramparts and whoop, and hooray,
And act in a most reprehensible way.
He did it quite often, as well as to choke
The Heavenly host with the vilest of smoke.

But up to the present St. Peter retained
His keys and his office, and Michael had gained
But little except the permission to hang
The notice forbidding his smoking his whang *
Inside of the gates; and the Archangel knew
That the saint had a pull, which, if he overthrew,
He would have to bring evidence, lucid and clear,
To prove that below in his earthly career
He was hardly so saintly as everyone thought.
And so through the pages he carefully sought
For data sufficient to make a good case.
And found that the saint was an impious, base
And hardened old hypocrite up to his death;
And only, in fact, with his very last breath

* Tobacco.

15

Had gabbled the prayer which allowed him to dwell
For the future in Heaven instead of in Hell.

His end had been sad.   He had stolen the pay
Of a soldier of Rome and had gone on his way
Pursued by the soldier, who won in the race,
And dealt him a terrible blow with his mace,
Which brought him to earth with a broken back-bone.
(And thus had the soldier recovered his own.)
But Peter expressed his emotions in prayer
Interlarded with curses that blistered the air.
And the bystanders wagered some trifling amounts
As to which he would make up his mind to renounce—
His prayers or his curses; for this would foretell
Just where he was going to, Heaven or Hell.

But Peter was lucky; his last moment came
As he wound up a prayer and before he could frame
A new malediction; and Heaven rejoiced
With exceeding great joy, and the glad tidings voiced
That the sheep which was lost had returned to the fold;
While the soldier, who'd bet on it, doubled his gold.

16

When Michael had finished this story, he turned
To the place where it told how the incense had burned
Some centuries later, when Rome was ablaze
With pageant and pomp of devotional praise;
How priests had paraded in sanctified style,
And bells had resounded to Heaven, the while
Cathedrals were packed with the worshiping throngs,
Who listened to music, and anthems, and songs,
When Peter was sainted; and found it to be
But a scheme of the Pope and the Most Holy See
To elevate someone high up on a perch,
And raise enough money to finish a church.

And Michael remembered the time it occurred,
And the trouble that Peter had caused when he heard
That down on the earth he was sainted.   He went,
To celebrate properly such an event,
On a tipsy carousal with Gabriel's horn,
Which he stole from the trumpeter; this he had borne
To the portals of Hell, and with blast upon blast
Had awakened the echoes of Hell, till at last   ·

He was caught by the devils, put under restraint,
And Heaven had ransomed its newly made saint.

He closed with a sigh; he could find nothing newer
Pertaining to Peter, and though he was sure
That Hell contained people much better than he,
The fact that the Pope and the Most Holy See
Had made him a saint put it out of his power
To question his claims to his Heavenly dower;
For papal authority governed his own,
And often exceeded the pow'r of the Throne.
And Michael, though premier and chief in command,
Had little control over such of the band
Of saints as held office, and this but increased
His wish to have Peter disrated at least.

As to why he was given the care of the keys—
It was one of the high and mysterious decrees
In which the Archangel had not had a voice.
'Most everyone thought that the Pope had the choice.
Be this as it may, the appointment had been
The source of a deep and most painful chagrin

18

To the rest of the saints, and it almost had brought
The most of them down to a point where they sought,
By prying and spying and telling of tales
And pitiful dwelling on smallest details,
To oust the old man from his saintly estate
And have him relieved from the care of the gate.

As he thought of the matter the message arrived;
From which the Archangel on hearing derived
Some hope that the saint had committed an act
That proved him so utterly lacking in tact,
So grossly incompetent, silly and weak,
As might make occasion of which he could speak,
And have the "old rascal reduced to the ranks,"
Where he could control him and punish his pranks.

He concluded to carefully watch, in the hope
That by giving the stranger a good deal of rope
He would probably hang himself; then, he could make
A greater display of St. Peter's mistake.
So he sauntered around to obtain a good view
Of the stranger, who soon hove in sight with his new

And splendid equipment, and Michael had gazed
But a moment upon him, quite shocked and amazed,
When he muttered: "He's got himself into a scrape!
"And the consequence this time he cannot escape."
And the joy that he felt was unholy and grim;
It was most unbecoming an angel like him.

The stranger passed on to the jubilant throng
Composing the choir.   As he hastened along,
His halo reflected the light from the Throne
And even surpassed it with light of its own.
His manner was dignified, measured and proud;
He carried the harp on his shoulder, and bowed
His head in devotion, and all had combined
To impress even Michael, who lingered behind.

So it is not surprising that all eyes were bent
Upon the newcomer as forward he went;
And the loud anvil chorus of praise to the Throne
That was filling all Heaven with thundering tone,
Intermingled with voices, and often quite drowned
By the twanging of millions of harps, and the sound

Of cymbals unnumbered, should cease and give way
To a murmur of voices and grievous display
Of wonder, and envy, and gross disrespect
To this latest addition to Heaven's elect.

The newcomer passed on his way undisturbed
And every expression of feeling he curbed.
He wanted a seat, so he sauntered around
And searched right and left; there were none to be found
Except one of gold, standing high and alone
And facing the choir, very close to the Throne.
He took it without hesitation, but first
Delivered himself of an eloquent burst
Of indignant reproval, in which he deplored
The reception they gave him; *the angels* encored.

And then he requested the choir would begin
An anthem of praise so that he could join in.
But not a sound came from that envious crowd
Except a low grumbling, not spoken aloud,
But which indicated, as Michael had guessed,
That discord had entered the home of the blest.

21

The sight of that halo in Heaven had made
A great deal of trouble, and I am afraid
Not one of that host could be joyful, unless
He also as well as the stranger could dress.

They threw down their halos, their harps and their books,
And gathered in clusters with envious looks
At the stranger's big halo; and all were agreed
That this did not fit into any known creed.
As lambs of the fold, they were heirs to the best
That Heaven afforded.   If this was a test
Of their faith and belief they had this much to say:
They did "not purpose to be tested that way."

So they grumbled, and growled, and endeavored to reach
A plan of concerted procedure.   A speech
Was made by a saint who advised that they name
A committee of saints and instruct it to frame,
And put into writing, a protest of this
Injustice to all who inherited bliss.
And others would settle the matter by force.
But none of the canonized saints would endorse

22

An open rebellion: they all had their say
But somehow they could not agree on a way.

It was a sad muddle, for should they procure
New halos for all of their number, 'twas sure
To establish in Heaven a troublesome, bad
And dangerous precedent; also would add
So much to the duties of Hell that the fires
Might suffer; and Heavenly justice requires
That sinners must roast—as in Scripture is told;
And besides, Heaven might get distressingly cold.

But should it so happen their claims were ignored
And the vials of Heavenly vengeance were poured
On their heads, as had happened long since to the band
Of strikers who tried to assume the command:
And they should be sent to the same horrid fate:
What triumph for Satan's malevolent hate!
For Heaven would have to start over again,
As Hell would contain all the spirits of men.

The outlook for Peter began to look tough,
And Michael now thought it had gone far enough;

23

So he quickly advanced on the stranger, who gazed
With indifferent eye on the trouble he'd raised.
He'd waited in vain for the music to start,
Then, saying that *he* would at least do his part,
Had tuned up his harp, and as Michael drew near
Had started some singing that ravished the ear;
So grand was the melody.   Softly at first,
Increasing in strength to a glorious burst
Of joyous devotion, this neophyte sang;
And divinely the voice and melodious twang
Of the harp seemed to mingle; and Michael stood still
And waited, and listened, until the last trill
Of the singing had ceased; for such music as this
Had seldom been heard in the regions of bliss.

But duty was duty; he must not give way
To his feelings, for here was the "devil to pay."
So he turned to the malcontents, crying: "Ye fools!
"Will ye let our Arch-enemy make you his tools,
"To depopulate Heaven and get the control
"Of the whole of your number, each saint and each soul?

24

"Behold here a foul emissary from Hell!
"From whence come the clothes that become him so well?
"From whence come that halo, that beautiful crown,
"And marvelous harp? Do you know that far down
"In the bowels of Hell, there alone is the skill
"To make such an outfit? In Hell is the will
"To conceive of this plot. *And in Hell is the lair*
" *Of this fiend who so daringly sits in my chair!*
"His purpose is plain: he has come to beguile
"Your eyes with his splendor, producing meanwhile
"Foul passions of vanity, envy and hate.
"Go back to your seats ere you find it too late!"

When he'd finished this short, comprehensive and most
Astounding oration, he turned from the host
And roared to the stranger: "Get out of my seat!
"Get out of it quickly! get up on your feet!
"Do you fancy that you are permitted to dwell
"In this place with your fiendish productions of Hell?
"Take off that big halo, that crown and the rest—
"You have brought such a smell to the home of the blest

25

" That ages must pass before Heaven is cleared
" Of the taint of your presence! Why have you appeared
" In our home? Did you think that we would not suspect?
" Did you think when you managed, through Peter's neglect
" Of his duty, to enter this sanctified place
" That everyone here had forgotten your face?
" *Declare yourself! Hell's Secretary of State*—
" DECLARE YOURSELF! BEËLZEBUB, SATAN'S FIRST MATE!"

When Michael had finished, the stranger arose,
And straight on the bridge of the Archangel's nose
He landed the halo. It fell with a whack
That laid out the Archangel flat on his back
Ere it circled aloft in a glorious flight
That rivaled the rainbow in color and light.
Then smashing the crown and the harp on the ground,
He bellowed a laugh of demoniac sound
And hid from the sight of them all in a cloak
Of sickening, nauseous, sulphurous smoke
Which came from his nostrils, and when it had cleared,
He then to the eyes of all Heaven appeared

26

A devil with pinions, hoofs, tail and the whole
Of the hellish equipment ; and blacker than coal!

A devil in Heaven!   O shame and disgrace!
A devil of Hell in this City of Grace!
No wonder the outfitting clerk is in bed;
No wonder that Peter now shivers with dread
As he stands at a distance and watches the row,
And mutters: "What's goin' to become of me now?"
For Michael had hit the right nail on the head
When, a moment before, in his speech he had said
That Satan had sent up his doughty chief mate
With orders to pass if he could through the gate,
And if once on the inside of Heaven he stood,
To cause all the trouble he possibly could.

And then when he got from the outfitting clerk
That order, he furnished the very best work
That Hell could produce, and the halo was made
By Satan himself, who had mastered his trade
When Heaven was building and Hell was unknown,
And he had the charge of the work on the Throne.

27

He remembered the halos in Heaven were all
Of a plain, simple pattern and made rather small;
And he knew what the outfitting clerk had not guessed:
That the halo he made would eclipse all the rest.

And Satan, arch-tempter, had never conceived,
Since Heaven had been of his presence relieved,
A bolder, a viler, more scandalous plot!
The job in the Garden of Eden had not
Been half so productive of sin and disgrace
As this, which had brought to this sanctified place
Such mischief; for when in the form of a snake
He tempted fair Eve in the garden to take
The apple, his wickedness only had been
The source of inherent, original sin.
And this had but hampered poor man on the earth,
And he still had the chance to achieve the New Birth.
But here was a plot which was meant to affect
The very existence of Heaven's elect!
For what could be done with a mutinous crowd
Of newly born, sanctified souls who allowed

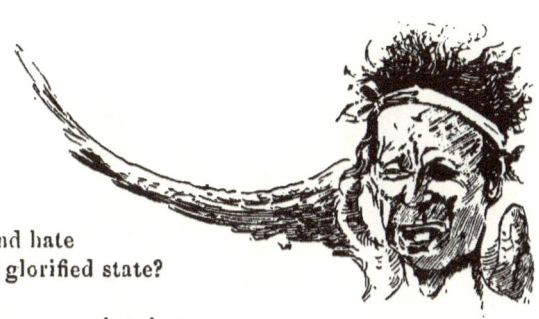

The passions of vanity, envy and hate
To 'rise in their hearts in their glorified state?

Great Michael lay prone for a moment; then 'rose
With a pair of black eyes and the bloodiest nose
That Heaven had seen since the days of the strike,
Quite sadly disfigured, and very unlike
The glorious Michael of dignified mien
Who always had kept himself tidy and clean!
With countenance bloody, and swollen, and flushed,
He roared to the angels to charge; then he rushed
On the devil, who mounted aloft with a grin,
And the angels pursued with the hideous din
Of the cries of the host in their ears, and commenced
A chase of a nature which only incensed
And worried the chasers, for, try as they might,
They could not lay hold of his devilship quite.

How this should so happen, I really can't tell;
But they were outflown by a devil from Hell.
The reason may be, that the devils had worked
While living in Hell, and the angels had shirked

And lain around Heaven with nothing to do
But daily to welcome a spirit or two.
And the watching of fires and the tossing of coals
With the details attending the roasting of souls
Will strengthen the muscles, and this may explain
How all of their efforts to catch him were vain.
He did not seem anxious to make his escape
Or to think he was caught in a very bad scrape;
For he dodged, and he circled, and led them a chase
That covered the whole of the City of Grace.
And they looked to the paralyzed legion below
Like so many pigeons pursuing a crow.

With faces perspiring and breath coming short
They probably thought it inglorious sport;
For little by little the weaker ones fell
To the rear and came down to the ground for a spell.
And soon the whole army, quite weary and worn,
Was scattered all over, and Gabriel's horn
Was sounded in vain; for it failed to arouse
Any great sense of duty; and wiping their brows

And holding their sides they returned to the place
From which they had started, and gave up the chase.

But Michael continued, with close at his hand
The trumpeter Gabriel next in command.
But vain were their efforts to capture the fiend,
Who laughed in derision, and dodged, and careened
To the right and the left with the greatest of ease;
And finally managed, in passing, to seize
The ankle of Gabriel; then he contrived
To swing him around, and the trumpeter dived,
While fruitlessly trying to turn himself 'round
By a furious flapping of wings, to the ground:
He struck; and stretched out with a gasp and a groan—
And Michael was left to continue alone.

Then Beëlzebub shrieked in demoniac glee—
'Twas heartless and mean to a shocking degree—
And Michael, enraged at his hellish delight,
Now roared a request that he meet him in fight!
But somehow or other the fiend didn't care
To meet the Archangel in battle just there.

31

He made him no answer: in fact he but grinned
And sailed through the air with the speed of the wind
To where old St. Peter was standing alone
And wishing himself a bit nearer the Throne.
And Michael, as Beëlzebub showed him his strength,
Pursued a short distance, then stopped and at length
Returned to his army, to muster them, for
He thought it was time for a council of war.

St. Peter perceived with increasing alarm
That the fiend now intended to do him some harm,
And started to run for the Throne, but he found
That the devil was beating him.   Down on the ground
He fell in his terror.   He screamed and he squalled
And loudly for help to the angels he called.
His cries were unheeded; the angels were now
In charge of their chieftain, who would not allow
A move to be made till the council convened—
So Peter was left with the terrible fiend.

He fell on the saint like a huge bird of prey.
But Peter by this time had fainted away

32

And could not feel Beëlzebub's clutch on his hair,
Nor hear his loud laugh as they 'rose in the air.
Just what he would do with him no one could tell,
But Michael remarked: "If he takes him to Hell,
"It will be a good job—we'll be rid of them both,
"And it's where they belong," but the devil seemed loth
To return to the region of clamor and crime—
He doubtless was having a very good time.

He easily carried his burden and flew
High up overhead, and when Peter came to
And awoke to a sense of his terrible plight,
And heard the fiend shriek in unholy delight,
And saw that the angels and most of the host
Away down beneath him were fully engrossed
In affairs of their own; then he moaned in despair
And made him the sign of the cross in the air.
He was dropped! and revolving and sprawling, he fell
While the fiend high above him gave yell after yell
Of malice and rage.   Then he flew to the wall
While Peter reviewed his whole life in his fall,

Recalled every item of trouble and strife;
And then disappeared in the River of Life.

The stream was beneath him, quite lucky for him.
And lucky it was, too—he knew how to swim.
He pulled himself out and lay down on the grass
To wait till his terror and weakness might pass;
And he bitterly thought how the angels and host
Refused him assistance when needing it most.
"It's all Michael's doings, I know," groaned the saint;
"He owes me a grudge, and I'm sure he will paint
"This matter so black that I'd best emigrate.
"I know I've turned people away from the gate
"Much better than even the best of that crowd.
"They wouldn't at least have kept still and allowed
"A devil to pounce on a helpless old man.
"But all of those people are under the ban;
"They're in Hell, and the discipline's very severe.
"Still, I don't seem to have any friends around here.
"They've kicked and complained till my smoking is stopped
"On the inside of Heaven—but why was I dropped?

"He was angry at something and gave me a toss.
"I have it! Why bless me! *the sign of the cross!*

"The sign of the cross! oh, why didn't I think,
"Before he came near, that all devils will slink
"And straddle their tails and run off in a fright
"When anyone makes such a sign in their sight?
"I'll stay where I am and hang on to the keys:
"I can handle the fiend just about as I please:
"But he won't approach *me*. As for that holy gang
"Who wouldn't assist me, why—they can go hang!
"They must think of the sign or they'll not get him out:
"And then if they don't, I'll be very devout
"For a while, till they notice the change in my face,
"And then I will chase him clear out of the place.
"Perhaps it will square me for letting him in,
"For I know I've committed a terrible sin."

So saying, he slowly went back to the gate
And sat himself down on his stool to await
The turn of events; while the angels and host
Were struck with his courage, but marveled the most

35

To see the fiend rise from his perch on the wall
Near the gate, where he'd sat since he let Peter fall,
And hover a moment, then take a short flight
To a place where St. Peter was out of his sight,
For the crafty old saint, with the cautious design
Of being *quite certain*, had made him the sign.
But Michael declared: "The old villain is full
"Of uncanny resources—'tis part of his pull.
"And notice: he fell in the water, instead
"Of a place where the fall might have broken his head."

Great Michael had been to the river and cleaned
The blood from his face ere the council convened.
A party was sent to bring Gabriel in,
But met him returning quite whole in his skin.
His fall had but dazed him and robbed him of breath,
And he still had a wish to be "in at the death."
The council consisted of Michael and most
Of his angels, and also some saints from the host,
Who down on the earth had perfected a plan
For casting out devils. The council began

And they talked, and they argued, but all were agreed
That to get him to leave them in peace they would need
Some stronger inducements than any yet tried.
'Twas useless to chase him; so they must decide
On some other method—but there was the rub:
No method there was to induce Beëlzebub
To return to his home in the regions below
Unless they were able to force him to go.
And Michael considered the shame and disgrace
And the danger besides to the City of Grace
In the making of terms: they might have to repel
In a very short time an invasion from Hell!

And Michael still thought, though the devil could beat
The angels in flight, should he stay on his feet,
They could catch him and bring the whole thing to an end.
Of course the success of this scheme would depend
On Beëlzebub's taking the very same view;
But this he was not very likely to do.
The council concluded the only thing left
Was a duel; for though of all honor bereft,

He surely would meet any angel of light
Who formally dared him to stand up and fight.
So Michael was chosen to challenge the fiend.
He advanced to the place where the devil sat screened
From the view of St. Peter, high up on the wall,
With his head in his hands and curled up in a ball.
But as Michael drew near him he gave a loud shriek
And passed overhead, and before he could speak
Had assumed the offensive; so, Michael returned
In a very great hurry.   The council adjourned.

For the terrible fiend was among them! He struck
To the ground every angel whose courage or luck
Would make him a victim.   He opened, full length,
Those hideous wings, and with marvelous strength
Now mowed through their ranks: to the left, to the right,
He dashed in his rage: it was useless to fight
This black incarnation of fury and wrath,
So all who were able got out of his path.
Then he turned his attention to Heaven's great host.
And Michael came up, and, on finding the most

38

Of his angels disabled and quite overthrown,
Disdained their assistance and chased him alone.

Those millions of glorified souls had remained
In the place where they stood when the premier arraigned
The fiendish impostor.   They noted his pranks
With some trepidation; a few in their ranks
Had patiently hoped that the trouble would end;
That glorious Michael would capture and send
The devil below where he came from; but most
Of that newly born, sanctified, heavenly host
Had talked themselves into a sad state of mind—
In a time of such trouble, 'twas rather unkind.

They claimed they were cheated; on earth they had been
Quite Godly, opposed to all manner of sin.
The church had attended each Sunday, and Lent
They had kept, and their time and their money had spent
To scatter the seed: they had humbled their pride,
They had fought the good fight, and at last they had died
In the odor of sanctity: knowing for this,
They were promised a future of glory and bliss.

But how were these promises kept? They had found
There were hardly good halos enough to go 'round;
The harps were worn out, as were also the crowns;
The robes were no better than shabby night gowns.
And now since they knew what the devils could do
In the way of fine halos, they wanted them too.
They wanted that devil put out of the place,
And at once; 'twas an outrage, a shame and disgrace
To allow him to stay and do just as he pleased!
And so they complained; but when Peter was seized
And dropped in the river, they grinned with delight;
And the saints all declared that it served him just right.

They were still of this mind when the devil had done,
With the angels; and now like a shot from a gun
He fell on their ranks, and there 'rose on the air
Such agonized wailings, such shrieks of despair,
As never were heard in fair Heaven before!
And Michael behind could accomplish no more
Than to climb over those whom the devil had struck
With his terrible wings, for with all of his pluck

And all of his strength, the Archangel now found
The fiend his superior, down on the ground
As he was in the air; and he paused in disgust
To wait till he'd sated his horrible lust
For battle, and then he might hope to induce
This devil to come to some sort of a truce.
But nobody thought in this general loss
Of resources to make him the sign of the cross.

And on went the fiend in his terrible might
Through the ranks of the host. 'Twas a sickening sight
As he felled them by dozens, with broad sweeping blows
Of his black horny wings, leaving rows upon rows
Of the stricken behind him: they scattered and fled
With loud screams of terror, and soon they were spread
To the uttermost bounds of the place, still pursued
By that demon of wrath. Before long he had strewed
The ground with nine-tenths of the glorified souls—
The other one-tenth had got into some holes.

But Peter was tranquil, quite tranquil indeed.
He had quietly watched the terrific stampede

41

With his nerves in command and his visage sedate,
Then passing outside through the heavenly gate
Went into convulsions of laughter: he tried
To stand on his head, but he failed; then he tied
Himself into contortions and rolled on the ground.
'Twas very unseemly and did not redound
To his credit; nay more, though I'm not very prim,
I think it was very disgraceful in him.

Then lighting his pipe he proceeded to smoke.
While inside of Heaven the angels awoke
To the fact that their troubles had only begun.
For in spite of the mischief the devil had done
He still was unsatisfied: up from the ground
He 'rose when he'd finished the host, and around
The Heavenly City he took a short flight;
Then all who were watching observed him alight
On the window of one of the mansions of gold
—The home of some glorified lambs of the fold—
There he stopped for a moment, then went to the next,
And in turn to them all, and the angels, perplexed

42

At his actions and wond'ring what now would transpire,
Soon heard from a distance the faint cry of "Fire!"

For the devil had opened each window and blown
A flame from his nostrils before he had flown
To the next; and brave Michael, on looking, beheld
A column of smoke from each mansion. He yelled
To the angels an order to run out the hose
And to man the machine, and he straightway arose
In the air with the purpose of forcing a fight
And straight for the devil directed his flight.
While the rickety engine was brought from its place,
And some of the angels proceeded to chase
The legion's uninjured from out of their holes;
For being short-handed they needed the souls.

The engine was placed and the suction hose dipped
In the River of Life, and the handles were shipped;
The hose was led out: the machine was then manned
By twenty-four souls who could not understand
How they were expected to do any work;
Still none of their number attempted to shirk.

43

And little by little the injured revived,
And battered and bleeding, by thousands arrived
To lend their assistance. They soon got a stream
On the scene of the fire, but the flickering gleam
Of the flames now appeared from each window and door,
And voices were drowned in the terrible roar
Of the pitiless fire, as it fiercely devoured
Their homes and their treasures and over them showered
A hot rain of cinders, while high overhead
The smoke in great volumes belched upward and spread.

They labored like heroes; 'twas useless; the stream
That played on the fire was but turned into steam,
And soon every mansion that Heaven contained
Was smoking in ruins, and nothing remained
Of their homes but the walls; they were proof against heat,
But the ruin of everything else was complete.
Fatigued and disheartened they lay down to rest
And wished they were rid of their terrible guest,
And watched overhead through the smoke where a pair
Of specks were revolving and dodging in air.

44

'Twas Michael and Beëlzebub. Michael had failed
To reach him before he had finished and sailed
High aloft to enjoy what his devilish brain
Considered a joke, and so, almost insane
With rage at their helplessness, Michael pursued
But could not induce him to be interviewed.

And down at the portal St. Peter had stayed
At his post like a hero—no longer afraid;
No cowardly terror assailed the old saint;
He puffed on his pipe without fear of restraint.
He heard all the sounds of the trouble within,
The roar of the flames, the loud shouts and the din
Of the rickety engine; and often would rise
From his seat to look in at the fire; then his eyes
Would twinkle and glisten and sink out of sight,
And the wrinkled old face pucker up with delight.
Then the wicked old man would return to his smoke.
'Twas shocking, his joy at this terrible stroke;
And Nero, who fiddled when Rome was destroyed,
To my way of thinking, was better employed!

45

At last it was over; he laid down his pipe
And muttered: "I think the occasion is ripe
"For my interference: a politic stroke—
"That sign of the cross; by its use I'll invoke
"The power that he fears; it 'll bring him, no doubt,
"To a state of subjection: I'll order him out.
"'Twill make me a hero and win the applause
"Of the heavenly legion, and maybe will cause
"Such a change in the ratings that Michael himself
"Will find that it lays him away on the shelf."

Just then from without, in the darkness, he heard
A voice, which in musical accents, averred
That its owner was "somebody's darlint," and too
"A wild Irish bhoy," and the gate-keeper, true
To his duty, decided to tarry because
This duty required that he knew who it was.
He had his suspicions, which soon were confirmed;
St. Patrick appeared, and as he would have termed
His condition, he had quite a "brannigan on!"
He hiccoughed out: "Pater, how are yez, ould mon?"

46

"How are you, friend Patrick," said Peter.   "And how
"Did you find it on earth?   Was there much of a row?"
"Wuz there much av a row?—but ye'd ought to been there,
"An' see'd the shillalies thot flew troo the air,
"An' the lashin's of whisky the bhoys histed in,
"An' the hids thot were broken!   Bedad, 'twas a sin—
"'Twas the siv'nteenth of March—but Oi s'pose ye know thot,
"Me birth-day, ye know, they paraded an'—Fwat!
"Fwat's thot ye say, Pater, a divil inside?
"A divil in Hiven! but why does he bide?
"They can't git him out?—go along wid yez now—
"Ye doan't mane to tell me thot no one knows how?

"An' the angels can't cotch him—bad cess to them all:
"They're of dom'd little use—so he guv yez a fall—
"The murtherin' divil; an' fwat is his name?
"It's Beëlzebob, is it? Oi'm glad thot Oi came.
"Oi chased all the snakes out av Ireland, begob;
"An' now Oi'll go in an' evict Beëlzebob!
"Fwat, Hiven afire an' the mansions all burned!
"Oh, where is thot divil? it's toime he returned

47

"To the Hell he belangs to; jist open the gate!—
"Oi'll play such a tune wid me shtick on his pate
"As 'll make him think twoice about comin' agin:
"Unlock the gate, Pater, an' let me git in.
"Doan't talk av the danger; sure, mon, ye kin boss
"All the divils in Hell wid the sign av the cross."

"No, Patrick; don't think of it—don't you go near
"That terrible devil—just stay with me here
"Where you're safe from all harm; you cannot subjugate
"The fiend with the sign of the——" "Opin the gate!
"Opin it, Pater, Oi ax yez." "No, no;
"You don't know the strength of our terrible foe.
"Just think of it, Patrick, he'll treat you the same
"As he did all the rest of us; I am to blame:
"Let me take the risk." "Will yez open thot gate!·
"Yez talk like a phool! must Oi stand here an' wait
"Till ye finish yer jaw whin me dooty requires
"Thot Oi sind the fiend back to attind to his fires?"

"But, Patrick, just listen, please listen to me——"
"Hush! hold yer whist, Pater, an' git out thot key!
48

" Yer almighty fearful, Oi think, all at wance,
" Thot Oi'll git into trouble: Oi'll batter yer sconce
" Wid me bit av a shtick if ye doan't let me in.
" Cóme open thot gate, ye ould skinful av sin!"
" No, Patrick, I wont, it is foolish of——"   " Biff!"
The stick of St. Patrick descended, and if
The head that it struck had been softer, 'tis clear
The blow would have finished St. Peter's career.
But the stick flew in pieces, then hammer and tongs
The saints went to fighting.   Such conduct belongs
To the regions of Hell; I, in fact, do not care
To describe the details of this shocking affair:
A very disgraceful proceeding; forsooth,
I speak of it only for love of the truth!

We return to brave Michael who, high in the air,
Was gnashing his teeth in his rage and despair
At the thoughts of the awful destruction and woe
And his impotent efforts to close with the foe.
For in battle he felt he was able to cope
With the powerful fiend; and a glimmer of hope

Enlivened his heart as he saw him extend
To the utmost his sable-hued wings and descend
In a narrowing spiral.   And so he pursued.
And Beëlzebub, finding the cha·e was renewed,
Now furled the broad pinions; then Michael the same;
And down like the rush of a tempest they came,
Pursued and pursuer, until 'midst the sound
Of the thrashing of pinions, they stepped on the ground.

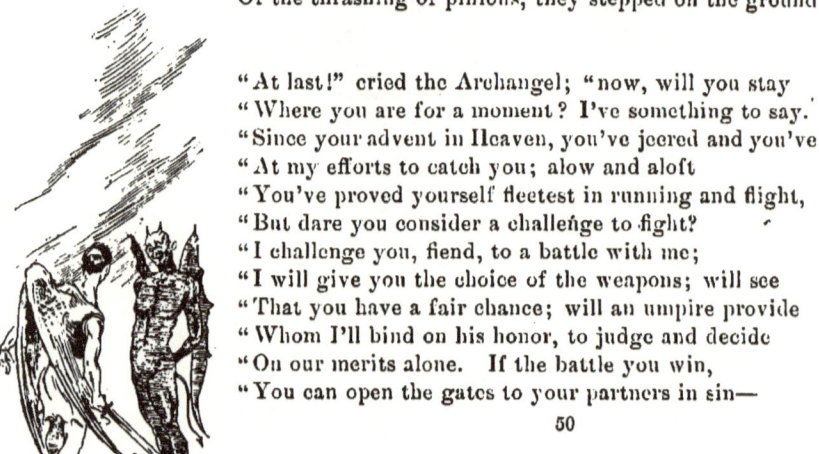

"At last!" cried the Archangel; "now, will you stay
"Where you are for a moment? I've something to say.
"Since your advent in Heaven, you've jeered and you've scoffed
"At my efforts to catch you; alow and aloft
"You've proved yourself fleetest in running and flight,
"But dare you consider a challenge to fight?
"I challenge you, fiend, to a battle with me;
"I will give you the choice of the weapons; will see
"That you have a fair chance; will an umpire provide
"Whom I'll bind on his honor, to judge and decide
"On our merits alone.   If the battle you win,
"You can open the gates to your partners in sin—
50

"You can turn what is left of our home into Hell
"And we in your regions of darkness will dwell.
"If I, on the contrary, prove myself best;
"You will merely retire from the home of the blest
"Without further punishment: *fiend, do you dare*
"*To meet me in fight? on the ground, or in air?*
"*With fists, wings and swords, knives and clubs, I'm adept—*
"My challenge is broad enough—DARE YOU ACCEPT?"

The Heavenly army had drawn very near,
Though the glorified legion hung back in the rear,
And Beëlzebub listened with dignified mien
And civil behavior, and, lo, it was seen
That a change had come over the devilish face.
It now was replete with a courteous grace.
The features had lost the demoniac grin,
The eyes had a kindlier light, where had been
That hateful, revengeful, malevolent glare;
And, raising his hand, he said, "Michael, I dare—

"Yes, Michael, I dare, but will not," said the fiend.
"Do you think that the passing of ages has weaned

51

"This heart from the love that once sweetened our lives?
"No, Michael, that love is still strong; it survives
"The pain and the anguish attending my fate,
"And you alone, friend, are exempt from the hate
"That I feel for your army. Think you I forget
"That battle, when wounded and sorely beset
"By your comrades, you saved me and bandaged my hurt
"And begged me to join you? I could not desert
"My captain; my love was less strong than my pride;
"But I never forgot it; and then, when the tide
"Of the battle had turned, and you sent us to Hell,
"There were tears in your eyes as you bade me farewell.
"No, Michael; I'll fight your angelic command,
"But against my old friend I will not raise my hand."

"You're hardly consistent," said Michael; (he felt
Of his nose as he spoke) "for you struck me a welt
"With your halo that shouldn't have come from a friend;
"I still wish to fight and my honor defend;
"My challenge is good; will you fight me?" "No, no,"
Said Beëlzebub; "rather I'll journey below

52

"And leave you in peace: as for laying you out,
"I didn't think clearly what I was about,
"And perhaps underrated the strength of my arm.
"I really am sorry I did you this harm.
"But in battle between us, to me it is plain
"That you would be worsted: I spare you this pain."

"But, tell me," said Michael, "just why you are here;
"Are you coming again with your crowd in your rear?"
"No, Michael, you're safe from invasion; in fact,
"There's nothing in Heaven to tempt or attract
"A well-seasoned devil; we're used to our Hell,
"And wouldn't feel anxious to come here and dwell.
"My object in coming is harder to state:
"My orders were merely to pass through the gate;
"Then send for an outfit and worry your host:
"You spoiled it or Hell would have had them to roast.
"That's all that I came for; Hell's where they belong—
"For, Michael, your scheme of salvation is wrong.
"But, when you denounced me, resuming my shape,
"And finding it easy to make my escape,

53

"I stayed to amuse myself; now, as for that—
"Your angels, I think, are a little too fat.

"They're sadly in need of more discipline, too;
"You cannot depend on so lazy a crew.
"If I had them in Hell, I could possibly make
"Fair soldiers of them; which I'd do for your sake,
"Although I'd be tempted to kick, I admit,
"The whole of them into the bottomless pit.
"And, now, in regard to the mansions I've burned,
"I'll speak to my master when I have returned;
"No doubt he will send some mechanics to build
"And furnish new houses, and see they are filled
"With treasures enough to fit out a full score
"Of the millions of souls you've provided before.

"Now, Michael, good-by, I am going!" "But stay,"
Said Michael, "a moment, and tell me, I pray,
"Your reasons for saying our glorious scheme
"Of salvation is wrong; do you know you blaspheme?"
"Most likely I do," said the fiend; "but I claim
"Your glorious scheme is a farce, just the same;

54

"Absurd and ridiculous!   Down on the coals
" Are writhing in torment the noblest of souls;
" And some are immersed in the sulphurous lakes;
" And others are prey to the goblins and snakes—
" All screaming and gasping; yet, what was their crime?
" They did not believe in the creeds of their time.
" Philosophers, scientists, teachers of men,
" Whose intellects soared to the uttermost ken
" Of human perception, who learned but to tell
" Their knowledge to others, are banished to Hell.

" And up here in Paradise, what have you got?
" Just look at them yonder; it's likely as not
" They're growling for outfits all 'round as before;
" I'm almost inclined to go through them once more.
" Yes, Michael, you're getting the worst of the game.
" Your glorious scheme is remarkably lame
" In its final results, though I do not insist
" That Hell gets the pick and the flower of the list.
" No doubt you have some, who in spite of their creed
" Have lived but in virtue and goodness of deed.

"But I mean that the greatest of scoundrels, who mark
"Their lives with the murderous tricks of the shark,
"On feeling the chill of the presence of death
"Can shriek out their fear with their fast failing breath,
"And begging for mercy from something unknown,
"Can die and your scheme will their baseness condone.
"You call it repentance! to me, it is clear
"It is nothing but ignorant, cowardly fear."
"That's so," said the Archangel, scratching his chin,
"For that is the way that St. Peter got in.
"Say, Beëlzebub, Heaven can do very well
"Without the old villain; please take him to Hell."

"Excuse me," said Beëlzebub, making a bow,
"You'd better keep Peter just where he is now.
"He's backed by the power of the Church and—hello!"
Just then a commotion was seen in the row
Of listening angels. St. Patrick appeared
In a very excited condition; he cleared
At a bound the short distance of space that remained,
And raising a hand that was bloody and stained,

He made ere the wondering fiend was aware,
The puissant sign of the cross in the air.

The inmates of Heaven were not in a state
To care much for anything, little or great;
But what now occurred was sufficient to cause
Their faith in their senses to waver, because
Of the wondrous effect of the sign on the fiend.
He tremblingly lowered his head till he'd screened
His eyes from the pantomime; then, a low whine
Came whimpering forth and he turned; but the sign
Was repeated right under his nose; then he fell
On his face, giving vent to an agonized yell;
Then Michael, astonished, endeavored to speak,
But his words were submerged in an ear-splitting shriek!
For the wrathful St. Patrick now pressed the attack
And traced the great sign of the cross on his back.

And a murmur of wonder arose on the air
From the angels and host, as the shrieks of despair
Rang out over Heaven.   St. Patrick now placed
His foot on the neck of the fiend he'd disgraced.

And standing in tatters, bespattered with mud,
His knuckles disjointed and covered with blood
(The blood was acquired from the gate-keeper's nose),
His features disfigured, one ear in repose,
One eye flashing fire and the other closed tight—
He looked like a typified genius of fight.

The puzzled Archangel now tried to induce
The saint to desist, but he found it no use.
He met him with volleys of stinging reproach,
And seeing the wondering angels approach,
He roundly abused them.   I cannot repeat
The language he used; it would sully my sheet.
But when he had finished the torrent of scorn
He shouted to Gabriel: "Gimme thot horn!
"Gimme thot inshtrument—gimme it quick;
"He nades a good batin'. Oi bruk me old shtick
"On the head of St. Pater before Oi got in—
"Jist gimme thot bugle; Oi want to begin!"

And, seizing the horn from the trumpeter's hand,
Who gave it in spite of the leader's command,

He yelled to his victim, "Come, git out of this!
"Yev been lang enough in the ragions of bliss."
"Hold on!" said the Archangel.   "Patrick, don't strike
"The fiend when he's down, it is—"Hold your tongue, Mike!"
"An' doan't interfere wid me; Oi'm me own boss—
"Ye'd better go practice the sign of the cross!"
A most disrespectful and impudent speech.
But Patrick, like Peter, was out of the reach
Of Michael's authority; hence he was forced
To witness a scene he would not have indorsed.

St. Patrick, now grasping the tail of the foe
And jerking him upward, delivered a blow
On his head with the horn; then he shouted, "Git out!"
And away went the twain, while a jubilant shout
Went up from the host.   He continued to whack
The terrified fiend on the head and the back
('Twas hard on the trumpet), and straight for the gate
The tandem rushed on at a furious rate.
And often the fiend would endeavor to 'rise
And as often the saint, with a growl of surprise,

Would hang his whole weight on that suffering tail
And cause such a plan of escaping to fail.
Yet he might, even so, have got out of the place
But Heaven's great portal was slammed in his face.

St. Peter was terribly thrashed in the fight,
And this is the way that he vented his spite.
For Patrick had let himself in with the key,
And Peter had left the gate open to see
What happened; and now, as the devil drew near,
With Patrick made fast to the tail in the rear,
In frenzy of rage and unsaintly chagrin
He closed Heaven's portal and locked the fiend in.

Then Heaven's great legion came down with a rush,
All shouting and howling; they met in a crush
Surrounding the two, where they struggled and fought
To reach the discomfited fiend who had brought
Such trouble upon them. The first who arrived
Were jammed into the center; the nearest contrived
Some blows to deliver, though not very true
(St. Patrick got most and the devil a few),

60

And others climbed over the heads of the rest;
Each making the sign of the cross on his breast.
And around in a zizgag the center was borne
With Patrick still pounding the fiend with the horn.

The angels themselves would have led the assault
But Michael had thundered the order to halt.
They obeyed, and their leader looked on in disgust.
"He spared me," he muttered, "through friendship and trust;
"And now he is weak and a prey to the wrath
"Of that pack of wolves: I will make him a path"—
And spreading his pinions, he soon was above
The struggling exponents of kindness and love,
Where, gauging his distance, he dropped to the ground
And elbowed a circle of space close around
The merciless saint and his victim: he held
His fist to the nose of St. Patrick, and yelled
"Let go of that tail and that horn—*I insist !* "
"Will ye moind yer own business ?" said Patrick.   The fist
Drew back and returned with the sickening crash
Of a battering ram on the jaw of the rash

And unhappy St. Patrick, who, dropping the horn
And the tail, by the terrible impulse was borne
Full forty feet off where, unconscious, he lay
Along with three others who stood in the way.

Bruised, bleeding, and sore from the blows of the saint,
The devil, released from the galling restraint
Of the weight on his tail, now arose in the air
And painfully flew to the battlements, where
He paused to recuperate: silent and glum,
He scanned them; then beckoned the premier to come.
So Michael, to hear what the devil would say,
Approached—all before him got out of his way.
"You'd better escape before Patrick comes to,"
He yelled, "and now, Beëlzebub, what can I do?"

"Friend Michael," said Beëlzebub, "ere I depart,
"I wish to express from the depths of my heart
"My sense of the debt I lie under to you;
"And also, I wish to apologize, too,
"For insulting you so, when I proudly declined
"Your challenge to fight; I have now changed my mind.

"But not with a wish to accept it—oh, no!
"I merely congratulate you on the blow
"That you dealt with such force on that terrier's head;
"He nearly had pulled out my tail as he sped.
"'Twas awful, and never in Heaven or Hell
"Have I seen such a blow and delivered so well.
"Still, Michael, admitting you're best in a fray,
"I think I could beat you in running away.

"Now, Michael, observe the condition I'm in;
"Contusions and bruises all over my skin;
"My strength and my courage departed, so weak
"That only by effort I'm able to speak.
"*But I fell by a power that is greater than yours;*
"*A power which on earth by its system immures*
"*Its hapless adherents in darkness and gloom.*
"*The foe to all knowledge and learning; the tomb*
"*Of more of the lore of the children of men*
"*Than all of its strength can enliven again—*
"*Which, octopus-like, having clutched in its grip*
"*The nations of earth, now endeavors to slip*

"An arm into Heaven.   Beware of that band
" Of canonized saints who defy your command!
" Beware of this foe to all human research!
"BEWARE OF THE POWER OF THE CATHOLIC CHURCH!!
"BEWARE!!! *or in time you will cower and crouch.*
"An ignoble slave to your saints who will—OUCH!!!"

The closing remark in this blasphemous speech
Was caused by his having endeavored to reach
His sadly demoralized tail to the front.
No doubt to gesticulate with, as is wont
Among devils when making their speeches in Hell.
For the wave of a tail will embellish and swell
A commonplace speech to a point where the gist
Is apparent without even shaking a fist.
The movement was painful; he tenderly placed
The tail in the rear, and on turning he faced
Besides the astonished and mystified chief
Another—a sad apparition of grief.

St. Peter it was, scarcely able to walk,
Whose appearance had now interrupted the talk.

But so badly disfigured, and battered, and bruised,
So bloody and dirty, so crippled, contused
And utterly woe-begone, helpless and faint,
That Michael himself didn't know the old saint.
Since shutting the gate he had seen what occurred
And, though at some distance, he even had heard
The sound of that terrible blow on the jaw
That ended the row; and he thought that he saw,
Inasmuch as St. Patrick was out of the way
And the angels and host were disposed to delay,
An opportune chance to fulfill his design
Of scaring him out of the place with the sign.

So he made the omnipotent sign with his thumb
—The rest of his fingers were all out of plumb—
But the fiend was a little more used to it now
And answered the saint with a courteous bow;
And without giving way to unseemly alarm,
He gathered the slack of his tail on his arm,
And then disappeared in the darkness without.
And Paradise rang with a deafening shout,

65

For at last they were rid of their devilish guest!
But many inquiries were cautiously pressed
On Michael regarding the speech on the wall;
But Michael maintained he said nothing at all
That really concerned them; in fact, he could vouch
That all that he said of importance, was —"ouch!"

So at last he was gone and the jubilant host
Returned to the choir, and the saint to his post.
St. Patrick was tenderly carried to bed.
In time he recovered, but found that his head
Was over to starboard; a permanent list
Was given his neck by the blow of the fist.
But he harbored no grudge, for in fact he admired
The Archangel's prowess, and even desired
That Michael would show him the way it was done.
He claimed it would furnish him plenty of fun;
And wanted, he said, to "hit Pater loike thot!"
'Tis needless to say the Archangel would not.

The gate-keeper also recovered his strength
And sang his own praise at consider'ble length.

He claimed that they couldn't consistently doubt
That he was the one who had made him get out.
But no one paid any attention to him.
So, seeing his chances of credit were slim,
At last he subsided and stuck to his post
And vented his spleen by abusing the host.

And the Heavenly host had endeavored to sing,
But couldn't somehow get the hang of the thing.
They sang out of tune, and they failed to agree
As to which was the meter and which was the key.
They started the chorus again and again,
But only to end in confusion; and then
They adjourned for a little to practice their parts,
They said.   But I think that in most of their hearts
Were traces of sin that they could not correct—
That halo had still its unholy effect.
They silently wandered, in pairs, and alone,
But took the direction the halo had flown,
And soon, lying under the southernmost wall,
They found the great halo, not damaged at all.

They tenderly handled the glorious zone,
And praised its remarkable color and tone
As they handed it 'round, but they couldn't agree
As to who was to wear it. At last a decree
From the Throne (or the Pontiff—they couldn't tell which)
Decided the matter without any hitch.
St. Peter was given the halo, until
The time should arrive when the devils could fill
An order for duplicate halos for all.
This happy decision averted a brawl.
And proudly the gate-keeper swaggered and talked
Of his value in Heaven. One night as he walked
Close under the wall, he was collared and dashed
Head-foremost against it: the halo was smashed.
He swore it on Patrick, but Patrick denied
The base imputation and loudly defied
His colleague to prove it, and wanted to fight.
Still I am inclined to think Peter was right.

And Beëlzebub proved himself good as his word.
One day a remarkable racket was heard
At the gate, and a covey of devils came in
With tools and materials, and, with a din

68

Of pounding and yelling, took charge of the place
And soon reconstructed the City of Grace.
And everything damaged was put in repair:
New outfits were made while the devils were there
(The halos were better than any yet worn)
And Gabriel managed to get a new horn.
And Patrick was happy; they voted him "boss,"
And he managed the fiends with the sign of the cross.

When the fiends had departed, the Archangel called
His angels around him, and having first hauled
The trumpeter Gabriel over the coals
For aiding St. Patrick, he spoke of the souls.
He called their attention to all that had past—
How ugly the saints had behaved, and at last
Repeated the terrible speech he had heard
From the top of the wall, and he even averred
That he thought every word of it true, and advised
Inasmuch as the power of the symbol sufficed
For the devils, that they in the future direct
Their energies closer to Heaven's elect.
And he said: "We will pay no attention to Hell—
"The Catholic Church can do that very well;

"But we must look out for the Catholic Church
"And keep it in shape, or be left in the lurch."

So, at Michael's direction the angels began
A course of athletics; they wrestled and ran,
They walked and they jumped, and they flew and they fought
With fists and with clubs till the Archangel thought
That his crew as policemen would do very well,
And promised to take them some morning to Hell
And show them to Beëlzebub.   Then a long club
And a helmet and badge and instructions to drub,
Recalcitrant spirits (at Michael's request
The devils had made him these things with the rest)
Were given each one; and patrolling their beats
They kept all the glorified souls in their seats;
And the host could now sing, and be glad, but—alas!
Saints Peter and Patrick don't speak as they pass:
A very unfortunate state of affairs,
Increasing a little the Archangel's cares.
And preventing me too, ere resigning my pen
From saying that peace was in Heaven again.

70